· LOOK AND FIND ·

Disney's

THE LITTLE MERMAID

Illustrated by Jaime Diaz Studios

Illustration script development by Christina Wilsdon
Lettering by Kelly Hume

Published by
Louis Weber, C.E.O.
Publications International, Ltd.
7373 North Cicero Avenue
Lincolnwood, Illinois 60646

Manufactured in the U.S.A.

8 7 6 5 4 3 2 1

ISBN 0-7853-0107-0

PUBLICATIONS INTERNATIONAL, LTD.

King Triton bids you welcome to his kingdom under the sea. It's a lovely and *lively* place, as you can see. Make yourself at home and take a look around. You may even meet Ariel, Triton's youngest daughter, who loves mischief and adventure.

Can you find these members of Triton's kingdom?

King Triton

Flounder

Ariel

Ursula

Sebastian

Arista

Lightning flashes and thunder crashes as Eric's ship burns and sinks. Alas, it is his birthday and his party is spoiled. But perhaps all is not lost! Can you help poor Grimsby find and save these birthday things?

For that matter, can you find and save Grimsby?

Eric's gift

A noisemaker

A party hat

A secret guest

Grimsby

Eric's cake

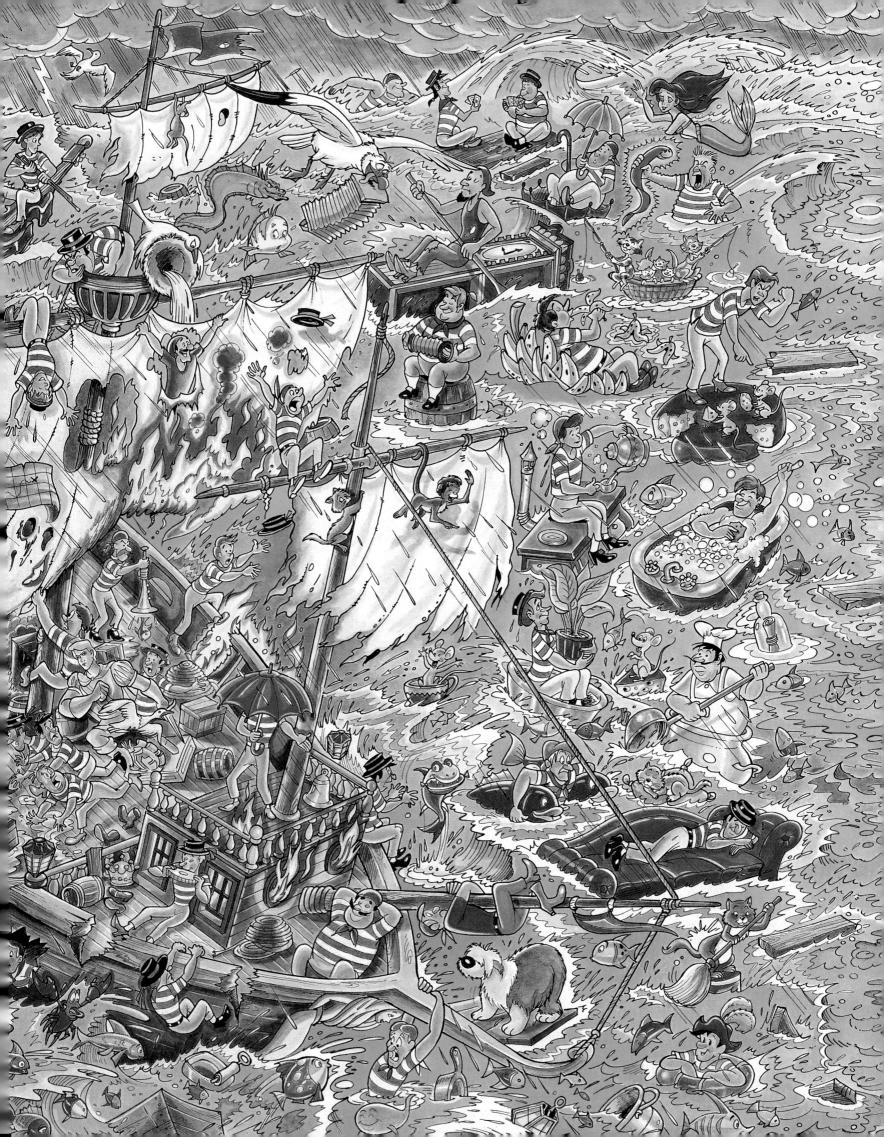

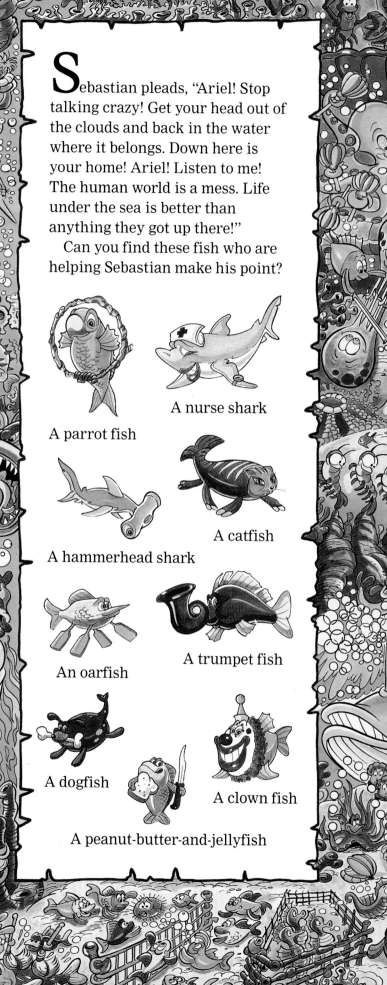

Sebastian pleads, "Ariel! Stop talking crazy! Get your head out of the clouds and back in the water where it belongs. Down here is your home! Ariel! Listen to me! The human world is a mess. Life under the sea is better than anything they got up there!"

Can you find these fish who are helping Sebastian make his point?

A parrot fish

A nurse shark

A hammerhead shark

A catfish

An oarfish

A trumpet fish

A dogfish

A clown fish

A peanut-butter-and-jellyfish

A riel has a secret hideaway where she keeps a treasure trove of human things she has collected from pirate chests and sunken ships.

Her intelligent friend Scuttle has told her the names of her prizes—but they are probably not the same names humans use! Can you find these amazing treasures from beyond the sea?

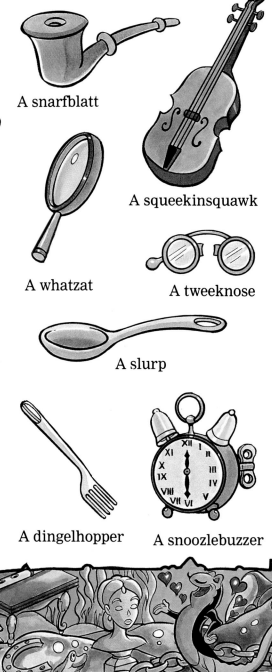

A snarfblatt

A squeekinsquawk

A whatzat

A tweeknose

A slurp

A dingelhopper

A snoozlebuzzer

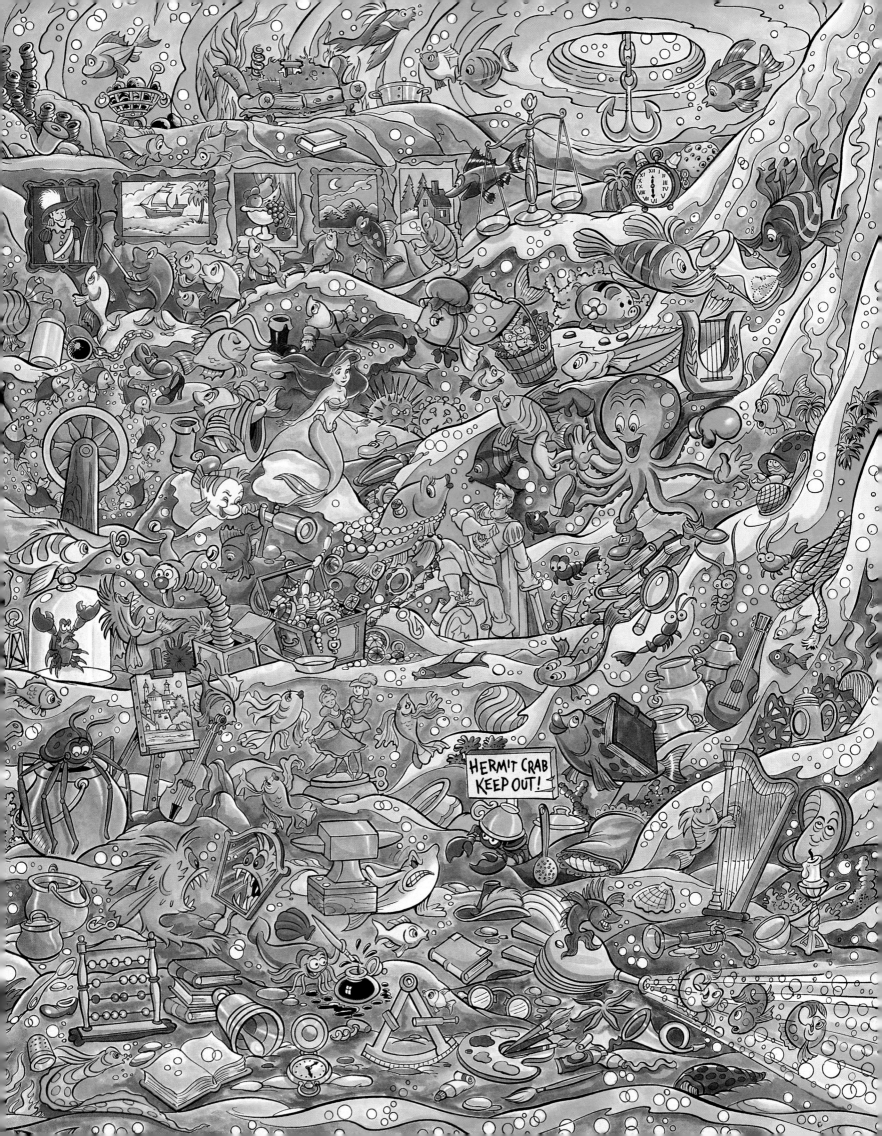

HERMIT CRAB KEEP OUT!

P oor unfortunate souls! Many merfolk ask for Ursula's help to grant their wishes—but the payment she demands is terrible indeed.

Can you find these wishful mermaids and mermen before awful Ursula gets her tentacles on them?

A lovestruck
mermaid

A starstruck
mermaid

An overworked
mermaid

An underpaid
merman

A scrawny
merman

An awkward
mermaid

Zoot alors! What is this? A runaway crab! He must be the missing ingredient for the special dish Chef Louie is preparing for Ariel tonight!

Hurry and scurry, Sebastian! Can you find these wonderful hiding places in the palace kitchen?

This watering can

This soup ladle

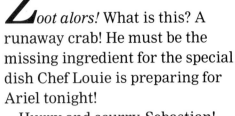

This teapot

This egg cup

This teacup

This cuckoo clock

The human world is a strange and wonderful place! Ariel hopes she can spend more than three days here. It is everything she had hoped it would be—and more.

Can you find the people in Eric's kingdom who are just as curious about Ariel as she is about them?

Chef Louie

The gatekeeper

The stableboy

Grimsby

Carlotta

The chambermaid

The gardener

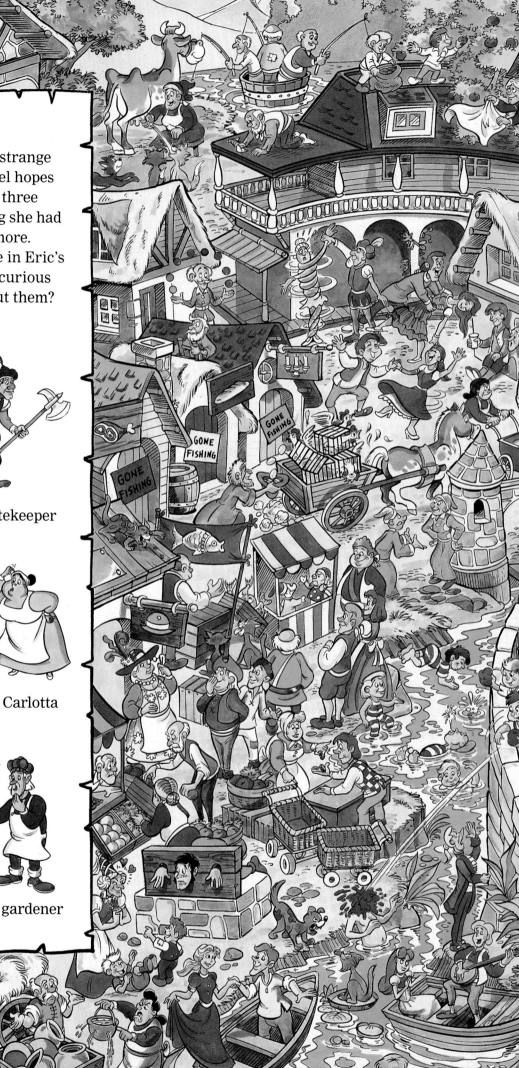

TAVERN

One kiss. That's all it will take to save Ariel from Ursula's evil spell. The lagoon is alive with music as everyone awaits the magical moment. So go ahead, Eric, *kiss the girl!*

There are three old friends among the serenaders tonight— and three old enemies. Can you find them all?

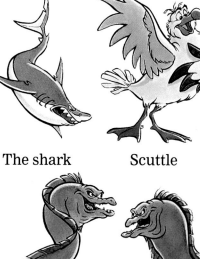

Sebastian   Flounder

The shark   Scuttle

Flotsam   Jetsam

Wish Ariel and Eric *bon voyage* as the sun sets on their wedding day. It is a celebration like none ever seen on land or under the sea! King Triton has invited everyone in his kingdom to swim to the surface to attend Ariel's fairy-tale wedding.

Can you find these guests who have come to wish Ariel and Eric a happy ever-after?

King Triton

Carlotta

Scuttle

Grimsby

Chef Louie

Flounder

Sebastian

Max

Go back to Sebastian's underwater orchestra. Can you find these instruments?

- [ ] A kettle drum
- [ ] A tuba
- [ ] A tambourine
- [ ] An accordion
- [ ] A triangle
- [ ] A harmonica
- [ ] Bagpipes

Go back to Triton's castle. Can you find royal subjects doing these things?

- [ ] Walking a dogfish
- [ ] Swordfighting
- [ ] Hanging out laundry
- [ ] Clipping hedges
- [ ] Jumping rope
- [ ] Teaching school
- [ ] Digging for treasure

Swim back to the shipwreck to look for these human things that Ariel is too busy to collect.

- [ ] A teapot
- [ ] A vase of flowers
- [ ] A ship in a bottle
- [ ] A clock
- [ ] A golden crown
- [ ] A treasure chest

Ursula has many kinds of magic. Can you find these magical things scattered around her lair?

- [ ] A crystal ball
- [ ] A book of evil spells
- [ ] A bottle of love potion
- [ ] A magic mirror
- [ ] An enchanted lamp
- [ ] A magician's hat
- [ ] A magic wand